Miss Alma May Learns to Fight

Stuart Rose

A Novella

Etchings Press
University of Indianapolis
Indianapolis, Indiana

This publication is made possible by funding provided by the Shaheen College of Arts and Sciences and the Department of English at the University of Indianapolis. Special thanks to the students who judged, edited, designed, and published this chapbook: Lindsey Henderson, Hope Coleman, Pamela Smith, and Adam Lourenco Fernandes.

UNIVERSITY *of* INDIANAPOLIS.

Published by Etchings Press
1400 E. Hanna Ave.
Indianapolis, Indiana 46227
All rights reserved

etchings.uindy.edu
www.uindy.edu/cas/english

Printed by IngramSpark

Published in the United States of America

ISBN 978-1-955521-01-7
25 24 23 22 21   1 2 3 4 5

Colophon:
The book interior is set with the Yrsa family
The cover is set in Josefin Slab and Montserrat

Cover illustration and design by Pamela Smith

Miss Alma May Learns to Fight

West Virginia, 1873

The brush beneath her feet crackled as Miss Alma May Jensen made her way down the hill towards the willow tree. The folded parasol in her hand was proving to be useless, unless she wanted to open it and be carried away by the wind. The young frost nagged at her toes, slowly soaking her second best pair of dancing shoes. Inside she felt like pig shit slipping down a mountain. Despair was an easy thing to settle into after two hours of sleep, especially on a damnably cold autumn morning. Miss Alma May fought it with fury, the rage boiling up in her chest. But despair was as hard to grapple with as a whole pile of slipping pig shit, so the fury and despair beget greater visions of each other as they tumbled and raged inside her. Alma May tamped it all down with a tight smile as she forged her switchbacks down the hill.

Her calves burned from her careful steps. All around her was brown, and red: the scrub-brush hillside so common to the western portion of the Virginias was losing its green, accelerated by the cloudy days. Hill, thought Alma. Near enough to be a mountain. Her cotton blue dress brushed the frozen scrub to either side of her. Her dirty blonde hair had come undone, nipping at her naked collar bones. Between the slippery slope and the mad and the bad fighting it out in her belly, she could take a tumble. Still, underneath it all there was a warm foretelling buzz in her, for the coming lesson. In the cold biting wind Alma allowed herself a genuine smile, before a breeze caught underneath her dress and swirled upwards. Alma gasped. Then she cursed. Then she continued down.

As she walked she thought of why. She knew the genesis of it all. Not that she needed him, not that she missed him, not that she wouldn't break his skull if his smiling face ever came by her place again. Damn him, and damn if it wasn't all too ten-a-penny to dwell on further. Alma grimaced. Every time she thought of Casper Fortune it was like someone taking a broken pencil and jamming it through her exposed rib-cage.

The sun was making an effort to rise on the eastern hillside, a burgeoning lightness amid gray. Alma turned to acknowledge it, and slipped on a little patch of mud.

She tried to steady her feet as the near-frozen mud took her down the hill in a way she did not agree with. Her heart missed a beat and her despair gave a growl of delight. She was skidding, flailing, the only thing stopping a full-on tumble was her heels digging into the mud. Alma gritted her teeth and fought for control.

She just managed to reach out and grasp the stalk of a withering flower before her skid took her off her feet. The stalk crackled and protested, but held. Once she was off the slippery patch she jammed the tip of her folded parasol into the ground and caught her breath. Alma examined the four-foot-high flower that had saved her. She did not know its name. Alma didn't like that, not knowing the names of things or what their true nature was. It had a bushel of thick green grass below it, a white hairy head releasing its seeds to the breeze. The bad boiled up in her chest; it followed the despair, always.

"Motherfucker," whispered Alma, and she bashed the flower with her folded parasol and continued down.

After Casper left was when it started. Or perhaps it had been there the whole time, just quiet. At first it was little things: an old picture that made Alma cry, seeing her boy begin to walk with the same saunter as his daddy and feeling only rage. At first she could control it. Bury it. Then things got worse.

Alma could just spy the top of the willow. She was pleased to see it was pink, and weeping: its branches formed a wild bushel and some dappled pink leaves clung to life despite the late-autumn weather. The willow was directly below her, tucked under the hillside's bulge a few hundred yards down. Still in the distance, especially if she wanted to get there in one piece. Alma forged her gentle switchbacks down, making careful steps as her mind searched for something to target. Anything to keep her from listening to her mad and bad.

The mad was the fury, the rage boiling up in her chest. The bad was the despair, the dark and bottomless chasm inside her. She couldn't remember when she named them. Alma whipped her hair out of the wind, her eyes on her careful steps. It was after she started feeling the need to retire to the closet and weep each night. It was before she broke that beer bottle and nearly jammed it down a customer's throat.

Alma spied another withered flower head just ahead of her. She bashed it as she passed. Was a man's deeds really at the core of her? Alma slammed her parasol against the ground and buried the thought forever. No, Casper was a hemorrhage just above her heart, not the heart itself. Alma looked for another target, but there was only herself and the weather. The scrub brush shook inconsequentially in the breeze. She thought of that pig-customer at her place, the one so close to the receiving end of the jagged bottle.

Alma ran the distinguished dance hall called Alma May's, herself being the sole owner and proprietor. The men-folk came each night and danced with one of her ladies for a nickel, and were encouraged to buy overpriced drinks and cigars. Alma moved among them and played the gracious hostess, dancing when she felt like it. The bustle suited her: in one glance, between grasping the arm of a new customer and laughing properly at another's off-color joke, Alma could determine which of the lot were getting too ornery, which were flush with cash, and just when she should start watering down the whiskey.

At first she loved it, being loquacious by nature. Alma ran a clean place, too: whenever a customer got confused as to what her ladies would do he'd be reminded with a firm kick to the testicles and directions to the nearest whorehouse. Paradox being a small mining town, there were only twelve or so to choose from. But most of her customers were looking for a drink, a dance, and a sympathetic ear. Most of them.

Alma shook her head in the breeze. The sun flashed light and was overtaken by the gray. She remembered the night when it all happened. It was a typical Monday, her place half-full. One of Paradox's least tuneful bands was playing, some of the men-folk were dancing with her girls, most were getting drunk at the bar. The clientele consisted of grizzled miners, a few fops, and cowpokes blowing through town. Alma had convinced herself she was getting better: she hadn't gone to the closet yet to weep, and when she felt mad or bad she just bit her lip and tamped it down.

Around midnight Alma felt the bad creeping up on her. She continued to smile among her customers, feeling that dark and bottomless chasm open up inside. The chasm whispered to Alma, told her it had always been there and was the natural state of things, and that to fight it was futile. It didn't help that a miner was talking her ear off at the bar, explaining the differences between igneous rock and sedimentary, and how his boss never listens to him.

Alma nodded in the miner's general direction, glanced at the closet between the bar area and the dance floor. Fat Suze was in there, putting away some cleaning supplies after an overexuberant cowpoke couldn't quite make it to the alleyway to part with his breakfast. Alma thought about what it would be like to pull Fat Suze aside, or any of her gals, talk their ears off about her problems. But Alma wasn't of that nature. No, the only one she could talk to about how much she hurt inside was the one that did the hurting, and he up and left. Alma felt the chasm grow inside her.

Through the band's off-kilter singing of "Oh Clementine," through the clatter of feet on the dance-floor, through the murmur at the bar, the chasm whispered to her. It would be easy: all she had to do was fall in.

Alma swayed before its might. Miles away at the bar, she heard a question in the miner's tone and nodded vaguely. She grasped the bar's countertop, the warm glow from the gas lanterns swirling. But the bad rose up, the chasm devouring her belly until it was empty black, and it was in her throat, and it was coming for her eyes.

Alma blinked back tears and bit her lip until she tasted blood. And then she felt it. The clenching of the stomach. The fluttering of the heart and her palms going sweaty. The mad rising up. Alma welcomed it, as fuel against the bad. She burned, the darkness inside her overcome with pure berserker rage.

She noticed the man then. Getting handsy with one of her girls. From across the room she gazed at his pig-face and his pig-hands as they reached behind the girl and squeezed. The girl was new, didn't know that the man's behavior was not to be tolerated. The two were standing kitty-corner from Alma, next to the stairs. The girl looked across at Alma with quiet, sad eyes. The pig-man looked at Alma and winked. Alma snatched the beer bottle the miner had been guzzling, broke it on the side of the bar, and stepped towards the man.

She stopped only when she heard the bare silence around her. Even the band stopped playing, the dancers rotating to a stand-still. All eyes were on her.

Alma blinked, coming back to herself. She glanced at the new girl, the pig-man's hands still on her. The girl looked as shocked as the rest.

"Oh lordey me, it looks like I broke a bottle," said Alma. "I apologize for that, especially to you, sir."

The miner whose bottle she stole burped, little suds of beer dripping down his tangled beard.

"The next round's on the house. I just need to freshen up. Let's have some music, boys. I'm not paying you to stare."

The dancing started up again. Alma smiled at the pig-man as she passed him, pointed him out to her bouncer as a man that needed to be bounced, went upstairs, bolted her door, curled up and cried in her bed.

Usually when Alma let herself weep she felt better after. But not that time. She didn't know why she did it. The mad had escaped her like never before. Grabbing that beer bottle had felt good, the glass smashing with a beautiful sharp quiver. Jamming that jagged bottle down the man's pig throat seemed like the most reasonable thing in the world.

"Tamp it down, Alma," said Alma to herself. The mad and the bad, and everything else too.

After a spell of blubbering Alma looked down and saw she was still gripping tight to the beer bottle, little shards all over her bed.

Alma was skirting by the top of the willow now. Just under the remaining pink leaves its bare branches were apparent, jutting out like daggers to all points in the sky. Alma liked that: the tree was slowly revealing its true nature. She imagined a certain man skewered on one of those sharp branches. He'd scream for help as he slowly sunk in. She'd be on the hillside, watching. The thought gave her a thrill before it gave her a shudder. More of her thoughts ended like that these days.

That night, after picking up the little broken shards, Alma had turned and tossed until she came to a temporary truce with her body, and she slept. The next day was Tuesday. That was Alma's shopping day. She had her dance hall girls to take care of, and her little boy. It didn't matter that she felt like five-cent coffin varnish, the mad and the bad still roiling inside her.

She and her ladies made a point of putting on their fanciest dresses whenever they could make it out of the house during the day. Alma strolled down the thoroughfare in her finest Henrietta dress, looking into windows, studiously ignoring the townsfolk's indignant and lustful stares, feeling mad and bad and without a thing to do about it, and that was when she heard the sound. It riveted her, right there in the middle of the thoroughfare.

That sharp *crack!* of breaking wood. Those animal grunts, coming from a man. People passed by her, but Alma was transfixed. The sounds were filtering up from between the false-front buildings on her left. And with the sharp *crack!* of the second or third piece of wood something cracked open inside her. She had to follow the sounds. She had to.

Alma left the bustle of the thoroughfare, headed down the alley known as sinner's junction. She heard the sounds again, a war-cry followed by a *crack!*, pursued them through another alley filled with shit and steam until she emerged and saw them.

Alma was almost to the bottom of the hill. She could only guess at why Mr. Liu had set the meeting here, two miles outside of the town proper, at the bottom of this in-auspicious conjunction of hillsides. She looked for them, but the base of the willow tree was still obscured. She descended, and the wind was gone. Some singing started, or perhaps it had been there the whole time. It was horrible singing, a plaintive off-key wail. Alma made a face she wouldn't dare let the singer see. Grating as it was, her ears latched on.

over seas and over mounnnnn---tainnnnnnnns
my body aches for dear May-Linnnngggg

I see her in my new-found daydreammmmmsssss
And when I wish she'll be with meeeeeeeeee

Alma saw flashes of the bare ground at the base of the tree. She saw flashes of a man, kneeling in front of the trunk. There was another man beside the one kneeling, straddling a low-hanging branch in the willow. The man in the tree was taking nips from a flask and beating his chest as he sang. The man kneeling was Mr. Liu.

Alma first saw Mr. Liu through a haze of steam, in that alleyway on that day. She smiled, in the remembering. She must have looked quite a sight, a soiled dove dressed to the nines plucked right out of the thoroughfare to gape at two men, two Celestials no less, punch and yell and break things with their fists. Mr. Liu's fists were bloodied, his chest heaving, broken boards scattered around him. Dumplings were cooking nearby, making the uncouth sight all the sweeter.

She watched them for awhile, half in and half out of the alleyway. They either didn't see her or had the grace not to call her out. There was such joy in their bellows, as Mr. Liu and his companion took turns pulverizing the boards with their fists. The splinters flew all over the alleyway. Alma was filled with a ravenous kind of joy.

And the first thing out of her mouth in that back alley was practically shouted: "Can I learn how?" And inside her there was a warm foretelling buzz, and the mad and the bad was quelled.

Alma was to the bottom of the hill. Both men were facing east, towards the rising sun. Alma was approaching from the west, their backs turned to her. Alma was glad: it gave her time to study up before they spied her.

They wore their traditional robes. So different from the men in Paradox. But what was she thinking…these were men from Paradox too. West Virginia men. Just of a different color. These were men who might've helped build the Transcontinental railroad, tough men, though they kept their toughness well-hidden. Alma could understand why.

Mr. Liu was small and sleight. Older. His long dark braided hair showed some gray. His companion in the tree was a barrel of a man, with strong hairy hands and power in his shoulders. His sandaled feet were hanging only a few feet from the ground, both legs unclad to mid-thigh. If this were Saturday night at her place, Alma would leave Mr. Liu with a bottle of her finest whiskey at a private table in the corner, then she'd dodder on the man in the tree, stuff him with all the food, beer, and female companionship she had on hand. She knew neither man would cause an iota of trouble; she also knew that, in a town like Paradox, trouble would likely find them.

She was close enough that her rustling dress could be heard. But the one in the tree did not stop his singing, and Mr. Liu kept right on kneeling.

All the brush had been cleared in a perfect circle around the tree. Alma paused at the edge of its clearing. She dropped her parasol and stepped into the circle. She tamped down her thoughts and gave Mr. Liu her best warm smile.

"Hello there," called Alma.

The singing ceased. Mr. Liu turned his head, just slightly.

"Well good morning, you fine gentlemen," said Alma. Now should she bow or should she curtsy? She'd seen these Celestials (was that the proper term?) bow to each other before. She decided on both.

"Miss Jensen," said Mr. Liu, rising in one fluid motion and bowing back.

"Please, call me Alma May. Or just Alma if you're in a hurry. Thank you for keeping our date."

Mr. Liu inclined his head. It was hard to imagine that this slight older man (was he in his fifties? Sixties?) could be so strong in body. But Alma knew that he was. Mr. Liu held himself poised, one foot forward, knees bent, shoulders back. His balance was perfect, and Alma was one to know. This man could dance up a rain storm at her place on any given night. The power, she decided, was in his eyes. They were dark and dancing, though the rest of his face was motionless. It made him damnably hard to read.

Mr. Liu's eyes flashed like he was deeply amused. She knew she was caught looking too long.

"You gentlemen found the only flat spot in all these rolling hills," said Alma. "And no brush either. I wonder how that was managed?"

"Practice," said Mr. Liu. "Now if you please Miss Alma, take off your shoes."

Alma hesitated. The ground was ice-cold. She complied.

Mr. Liu stared at her, assessing. Alma gave him her best: plumping her lips and flexing her dimples, showing off just the right amount of pearly whites. She raised her brows and widened her blue-gray eyes, giving the impression that she was deeply impressed with everything around her.

Mr. Liu's dark eyes flowed over her. Alma was damn good at reading people, especially men, figuring out their wants and desires, and if it was in her interest then giving it to them. But Mr. Liu's face was a carven mask. Though as he studied her Alma sensed a deep feeling emanating from him. It was like it welled out of his core, and he didn't do anything to stop it. And the feeling Alma sensed from him was disdain.

Alma's smile faltered. She felt suddenly naked, exposed, all the things she kept locked inside her flying out. Could he see her mad and bad? Could his dark dancing eyes ferret out her secrets, her wants, graze open all those ugly things inside her?

After a moment of despair Alma let a deeply gratifying thought wash over her: fuck him. She'd show him what her strong looked like.

Alma narrowed her blue-gray eyes. She threw back her shoulders, put one freezing foot back. She bent her knees, lifted her chin and sneered.

A smile just touched Mr. Liu's lips. "We have much work to do," he said.

Alma inclined her head.

"Would you like to learn how to breathe first, or walk?"

That caught Alma off guard. She bit back a thousand sassy answers. She was hoping to get right to the punching of things.

"Walk, I suppose," spat Alma.

Just then the sun came out in earnest. The man in the tree, whose singing had dropped to a low mumble, bellowed like he'd never seen such wonder. Alma smiled.

"Can I meet your friend?"

Mr. Liu gravely shook his head. "That man up there is no one's friend. He is a Korean dog who follows me around all day and all night."

"What lies you speak! I am a beautiful man!" roared the man in the tree.

"Quiet, or I will put you back in your kennel!"

The man in the tree went back to singing, spitefully.

"Please," said Mr. Liu, holding his hand out to her, "Walk to me and walk back now."

Alma, a little confused, did so. The ground was icy on her toes, but she knew better than to complain. She knew how to walk. She was a goddamned dancer.

"Ah. Terrible," said Mr. Liu, when Alma had completed her circuit and was back at the edge of the clearing. "You Americans don't know how to walk properly. I suspect it's your ever-larger heels. Always walk on your toes. Never walk with your heels. One walks with one's heels only to announce one's presence. You Americans always want to announce your presence. Walk to me and back again, using only your toes."

Alma hesitated. Was this what she got up so early for? Learning to walk? She wanted to break a wood board or two. She wanted to let the fury out.

Mr. Liu must have sensed her hesitation, for in that moment he slipped off his shoes and began to move. It was less like walking and more like pouncing. Mr. Liu's left foot was forward, his right back, his knees bent, his arms clasped behind his back. He traversed around the clearing, moving leftward and forward and side-to-side. Always his stance was steady: the only muscles he was using were in his toes. Alma liked that. His body betrayed nothing about his next movement. It reminded her of a big cat, the way he was pouncing and prancing. She was careful to guard her amusement.

"Do you see how beautiful I am moving?" said Mr. Liu as he pounced around the tree. "From here I can attack, I can retreat, I can duck and dodge. This is why."

"You look like a skittering rat," said the man in the tree, and he went back to singing.

Alma bit back a smile. Mr. Liu held out his hand to her, his dark eyes dancing. "Your turn."

She walked, her toes gripping the cold dirt, fast turning wet in the warming day. She tried doing little pounces on the way back.

"Not bad. Better," said Mr. Liu, stroking his hairless chin.

"Mr. Liu, I'm a dancer. I know all about moving my feet."

"Oh really? Then climb the hill. Head to the sun. Go straight, no turns. Use only your toes. Go now."

She bit back a thousand and one sassy answers. She bit back rage. Mr. Liu raised his brows, his arms clasped behind his back.

She left the bottom of the hillside without bowing. She made it about a hundred feet before her right heel collapsed to the ground. She kept going. The rage filled her, strengthened her. Once she was high enough she began cursing Mr. Liu's name. Her lungs were raw. The wind picked up. The sweat poured off her, freezing onto the back of her dress. Her left heel collapsed. Her calves were on fire. The rage ran its course, and all she was left with was pain. For once she didn't try to tamp it all down. Not that she could, with the rising ache in her legs and her lungs. Somehow the pain overcame the despair, all the mad and bad in her. Somehow it made her strong. Alma felt a thrill, a joy mingled with the pain. She climbed. After a while the sun started to warm her.

Alma took her time in walking back down.

"Did you touch the ground with your heel?" asked Mr. Liu.

"I did, Mr. Liu."

"Then you have failed. Hey, that's OK. Tomorrow, if you come, you shall try again."

"Tomorrow?"

"Tomorrow. Or did you think you can learn all there is to know about Muay Thai in one day? Before I teach you striking, before I teach you dodging, we must get you strong from the ground up. This is why."

She hesitated, then she bowed her head.

"Yes? What is it?" inquired Mr. Liu.

"Mr. Liu, it will be colder tomorrow. The sweat freezes to my back."

"Ah. Next time don't sweat. Or tell your feet to grow big thick hairs, like my Korean companion here."

The man in the tree wiggled his sandaled feet. Even from her place at the edge of the clearing, Alma could spy the man's thick black hairs sprouting from thigh to toe, two hairy drumsticks dangling from the branch. Alma couldn't look away.

Mr. Liu said in a stage whisper, "He tells me his hairy feet are much sought after in his land. And all the women chase him, so they can have beautiful hairy-footed children."

"It's so true!" bellowed the Korean man, and he took a gulp from his flask.

Mr. Liu clapped his hands together. "Now before our time is over, I will teach you a punch. You are not ready, but I want to be a good teacher to you, and I know that you Americans are very impatient, and you want to get to punching on the first day."

Alma gave him a nod and a wink.

Mr. Liu assumed his fighting stance. He put his left foot forward, brought his fists to his cheeks. "Now, to punch you need good legs, snapping hips, and a strong breath. The arm is the least important part of your punch. Mirror me."

Alma went alongside him. She felt that ravenous kind of joy. "Now strike with your left fist," said Mr. Liu. "Keep your right fist attached to your right cheek, to defend against sneaky attacks. Step out with your left foot as you strike. Snap your hips to the right. Turn your fist as it reaches its destination. And say *ha!* as you strike. Or you can give a growl, whichever you prefer."

Alma tried it. She did everything but give a growl or say *ha!*

"Ah, terrible," said Mr. Liu as he watched her. "But hey, that's OK. Perhaps first we shall work on your breath. You Americans don't know how to breathe. It is why you accumulate so much bullshit, I think. The bullshit hides at the bottom of your lungs. Now, we get it out."

"Okey-dokey," said Alma.

"So breathe in through your nose. Breathe deep."

Alma did, still in her fighting stance.

"Now when you exhale, do it through your mouth. "Say haaaaaaaa, like a strong hissing animal. Say it deep. Picture yourself as a cobra. Or a lion. Or, as my Korean companion does, a cuddly panda bear."

"Not true," sang the man in the tree, "Oh I am so much more, so much more than you think..."

"Your throat opens up as you let out your breath," continued Mr. Liu. "Picture a pipeline going from the bottom of your lungs to the back of your throat. You are opening this pipeline. And remember, you are not a person. You are a strong hissing animal. Which animal are you?"

"I'm a motherfucking python."

"Ah, very good! Pythons say "Hisssss..."

"Hisssssss..." said Alma as she let out her breath.

"Good. Now do it as you punch. Every time. Let's begin."

And so they did, as the sun rose and the leaves fell and the day slowly warmed. The two mirrored each other in their snapping hips and stepping feet and pistoning arm, she in her dress and he in his robe, Alma saying "hisssss" each time her fist moved toward its destination. The sweat on her back unfroze and flew off her. It was pleasing, her breath and her fist letting out little pieces of fury. The only thing spoiling it was the Korean man's song, so off-key it threw off her timing.

over seas and over mounnnnn---tainnnnnnns
my body aches for dear May-Linnnngggg...

"Oh, and by the by, what do you think of my Korean companion's singing?"

Mr. Liu had stepped out of his fighting stance, and was looking at her intently. Alma might have caught some amusement in his eyes. She sighed. On the one hand, listening to the song was a hell of two pots clanking together, and the mad part of her wanted to rip those dangling legs out of their sockets for daring to think the singing was welcome. On the other...

Alma bowed deep. "I think it is very beautiful," she said, and as the words left her mouth she marveled at how politeness breeds despair.

Mr. Liu smiled, and turned to the dangling legs in the tree. "Do you hear that, you Korean dog? She likes your singing! Sing louder, for the nice lady to hear!"

It was time for Alma to take her leave. By the sun's position she figured it was mid-morning. She had to go wake her boy. And make sure the house was up and running. And hunt down the sheriff, who was amassing quite a bar tab.

"Oh and as you walk back to town, do it on your toes," said Mr. Liu. "And remember to breathe like a python. Do this for the rest of the day. And forever, always, until your last breath. It will be helpful."

"Okey-dokey," said Alma.

"And tomorrow you shall awaken very sore," continued Mr. Liu, "You will remember that you have many important things to do, and you will not want to come here and train. The most difficult part about tomorrow will be making the decision to come here. Everything else is easy. We shall see, whether you have enough warrior in you to return."

Alma climbed. The eastern hill again. Behind her, the Korean man's song faded. The wind picked up. She cursed Mr. Liu's name.

Alma did indeed awaken very sore. It felt like there were two filled beer barrels pressing into her shoulders, and her calves were tenderized meat. Before she rose she lifted her blankets, thinking she had forgotten to take off her corset, for her ribs felt choked in on themselves. Alma glanced out her bedroom window, still dark and with delicate patterns of frost encroaching on the panes. She thought of how far out of town she had to walk, how cold she would be, and what was the point of it all again? The chasm opened up inside. Alma breathed. She cracked her knuckles. She wasn't no lily-livered sage hen. She climbed out of bed and made the journey, stiff as Lazarus risen.

As she walked down the hillside in the fading dark she marveled at how the mad and the bad was quieter today. Maybe the pain in her body had overcome the quarreling in her. Maybe all that punching yesterday had begun the release of it. And maybe she shouldn't be thinking about it so much.

The weeping willow was unloosening its tiny pink leaves in abundance. At the clearing around the tree Alma came upon the same scene as the day before, with Mr. Liu kneeling and his Korean companion singing in the tree. Only this time when she stepped into the circle Mr. Liu rose and pointed at the eastern hill, and kept pointing until Alma slipped off her shoes and started climbing. Next time she would just arrive barefoot.

It was harder to climb than yesterday. The tendons in her calves and thighs felt both taut and aflame, like lit dynamite wicks. The wind whipped her hair in all directions. No burgeoning sun to warm her today; the gray was infinite and uniform over the vast West Virginia sky. She made it almost half-way up before her heel collapsed. The skin on the bottoms of her feet were frozen. She kept on going.

"Did you touch the ground with your heel?" asked Mr. Liu, once she was back down.

"I did, Mr. Liu."

"Then you have failed. Tomorrow you shall try again. If you come. Now, if you were a soldier in my regiment in Si-chuang I would have you up and down these hillsides for months before I taught you anything else, and I would paint your heels to make sure you didn't cheat. But here in America I have grown soft at heart, and I want to be a good teacher to you, and also I know you are an American woman who is very impatient, so today I will teach you new skills. Attack me."

"What's that now?" asked Alma.

"Attack me. Punch my belly. Punch my sing-song face. Are you not a python? I thought you were here to strike. So strike."

Alma didn't budge from the edge of the clearing. Mr. Liu shook his head. "Ahhh. You are hesitant. Perhaps your hesitancy will get you killed someday. It is why I despise women. You refuse to act. You ponder and you pour over with feelings, but in the end you do nothing. This is your chance now, for action. Attack me."

Alma let the mad boil up inside her. It was pure and it was perfect, the fury moving from her belly to her fists as her knuckles cracked. Still she tamped it all down with a tight smile. It could only be a trap. The wind picked up, and a bushel of pink leaves blew across the space between Alma and Mr. Liu. The man in the tree was silent.

"Here, let me make it easier for you," said Mr. Liu. He walked behind the willow tree, produced an ax and raised it above his head. He let loose a war-cry and charged her.

Alma watched Mr. Liu run at her like she was the audience at some stage play. The ax-head glinted from a bit of sun. Mr. Liu had his mouth open, and she thought he might have been screaming. He closed in, only a few feet away. He wasn't going to turn. At the last moment Alma stepped out with her left foot, closed her eyes, snapped her hips and punched. She connected with something soft. She heard the ax fall to the ground, followed closely by a body.

When she opened her eyes Mr. Liu was on the ground beside her, and she heard laughter from the man in the tree.

"Very good!" said Mr. Liu. "When the time came, you struck."

She smiled and helped him up. "Did I hurt ya?" asked Alma.

Mr. Liu touched his left ear, which was turning purple. "A little. But I never liked this ear."

"Maybe the nice lady can punch your face into handsomeness, you filthy Chinese rat!" bellowed the man in the tree.

"Or maybe she can make me so deaf I can't hear your singing! Oh what a blessing that would be!" countered Mr. Liu. He turned to Alma, his dark eyes dancing. "I apologize for my derogatory remarks about women, Miss Jensen," said Mr. Liu, and he bowed. "I was trying to rile you. How does your hand feel?"

"Well, my wrist aches a bit. And my nails dug into my palm when I struck ya."

"Ah. I suggest you keep your nails trim. You can drop that modicum of being a lady, yes? And also you must learn to punch straight. Your arm is an arrow, straight and true. And also, you must connect your punches knuckle-first. You are kissing your enemy with your knuckles. And also, do fifty push-ups and one hundred squats, and then we can talk more."

Alma didn't bother to hide her sneer as she bowed. At least what fury she was feeling could be put to good use.

She got down on her knees and started the push-ups. Mr. Liu hovered over her, stroking his hairless chin.

"Also do twenty pull-ups on the tree."

Alma's cotton blue dress was covered in sweat and mud. She stood swaying before Mr. Liu. It was an interesting feeling, being so tired she could hardly stand. The mad and the bad were driven from her, replaced only with pain. She thought fleetingly of trying to charm Mr. Liu, of batting her eyelashes and getting him to go easy on her, maybe only doing ten push-ups on the next go-round. But she was just too worn out to flex her dimples and play the gracious lady. Also, she didn't want to.

"Now, we begin. Do you know the one-two punch combination, Miss Alma?"

Slowly, Alma gathered herself. "I do not."

"Ah. It is your butter and bread. Put your fists up to your cheeks. Elbows in. Shoulders back. You are wearing a mask of fists. I forgot to inquire, do you use your right hand predominantly?"

"I prefer the left."

"Ah, a 左撇子. In my country you would be...strongly encouraged to use your right hand. But perhaps America is rubbing off on me and I am becoming more liberal in my old age. If you want to use your left as your long punch, that is okey-dokey with me. Is that your wish?"

"That is my wish."

"Very well. Right foot forward. Left back. Your hips

are aligned with your enemy's, always. Like dancing, yes?"

Alma May laughed. "Yes, we just don't think of our dancing partners as enemies so much."

Mr. Liu's eyes danced. "Ah, you don't? Well then. You know your jab. That is your right fist. The two is your long punch, with your left. First one, then two. Remember the snapping of your hips. Remember your breath." Mr. Liu moved to stand before Alma, putting both hands palms-up to either side of his head. "Now punch."

Alma did. The sound made a satisfying slap against Mr. Liu's palms.

"Ah. Terrible," said Mr. Liu. "But that's OK. Don't flare out your elbow. Remember, your arm is an arrow, straight and true. With your other arm, you are drawing back the bow. But keep your left fist at your cheek, to defend against sneaky attacks. And remember to hiss or grunt or yell when your strike connects. You are not Alma. You are a python, yes? You are a striking snake."

Alma grunted "Hisss!" as she struck, the sound welling up from the bottom of her lungs. Mr. Liu's palm flew back. Perhaps he exaggerated the movement, perhaps he didn't. "Very good!" said Mr. Liu, and he smiled. The man in the tree hit an operatic note. "How did it feel?"

Alma found she was smiling. It was a strange feeling, not having to work at it. "It felt like I hoped it would."

"Good," said Mr. Liu. "Now do it five hundred times."

The sun was fully up, and it was time for Alma to take her leave. She bowed, and Mr. Liu bowed back.

"Oh, and tomorrow's soreness shall be much worse

than today's. You will remember today's soreness as a mild tummy-ache, and tomorrow's shall be a bone-breaker. You might say to yourself, I have completed my mission and am perfectly at peace, so why bother to train? Whether or not you have a warrior in you, we shall see."

After that Mr. Liu had her up and down hillsides for a week afterwards. No punching, only pull-ups and push-ups and squats. Each morning it was harder to rise, but she rose. Each morning when she came to the clearing she found Mr. Liu kneeling and the Korean man in the tree singing, the pink leaves of the willow weeping.

It was around the tenth day, when Alma all but crawled down the hillside, that Mr. Liu finally took pity on her, teaching her some stretching techniques to help with her soreness. Still she ran up and down hillsides and did endless rounds of pull-ups, push-ups, and squats. Always Alma walked using only her toes. Always there was pain. Always the mad and bad was inside her, but put to use now. The breathing helped the bad, the dark and bottomless chasm had a place to go. And the mad poured from her through movement, through the salt of her sweat. Still she wanted to feel the fury in her fists. Still she wanted to punch.

"I wonder if you will keep coming, Miss Alma?" mused Mr. Liu one day, when Alma collapsed to the cold hard ground after doing the required pull-ups. "I wonder if you have a warrior in you?"

But Miss Alma May Jensen knew what was good for

her. She hadn't felt the need to cry in the closet in awhile, and she was more patient with her boy too. It made her smile in her quieter moments, after she tucked her boy in or when she was counting the evening's take after a busy Saturday night. But always they were with her, her mad and bad. The worst was the mornings, waking up at dawn. That was when the chasm threatened to swallow her up. Alma beat it by outrunning it, springing out of bed before the bad could take hold, remembering to land on her toes. It worked too, just so long as she kept doing it. Still she wanted to punch.

She'd come down after dawn, red-eyed and riled and freezing her can off. Mr. Liu would rise and assess her. At first Alma tried to smile her way into it. But at the first twitching of her lips Mr. Liu would point at the eastern hillside, and keep pointing until Alma started climbing. Then she started getting pissed off. She'd feel it once his eyes were on her: the clenching of the stomach. The fluttering of the heart and the palms going sweaty. Old habit told her to tamp it down. The second she tried Mr. Liu would start pointing.

One day, a particularly gray and threatening one, Alma almost didn't come. The chasm nearly swallowed her, as she lay in her bed. Even with the stretching, she was damned sore. When pressed, each part of her body shouted agony. After all that training, Alma still felt them: her mad and bad. Wasn't she supposed to be better? Wasn't she supposed to be cured? Why couldn't she just punch away her problems and be done with them? Maybe she was as good as she was ever going to be, and she should just stop. Thus the chasm whispered to her, rising up.

Still Alma rose and made the journey, two miles outside of town, down the hill to the clearing, remembering to use only her toes. Mr. Liu and his companion were in their usual places. The willow's pink leaves were all but gone.

Mr. Liu rose and assessed her. Alma felt it rise up. This time she let it come. The clenching of the stomach, the heart fluttering and the palms going sweaty. Mr. Liu's eyes danced over her. Alma sneered. It felt good, to sneer.

Mr. Liu slowly raised his hand and pointed at the eastern hillside. Alma let out a particularly long breath, cracked her knuckles, and bowed.

Just before she left the clearing, Mr. Liu spoke to her back, "Oh, and when you come down you will do one round of pull-ups, push-ups, and squats. Then we can get to the punching."

Despite the cold, Alma smiled her way up the hillside.

And now her fists were on fire. She had discarded her cotton blue dress, in tatters after less than three weeks of training. Rain had started to fall, a gray and steady West Virginia drizzle. Clad now in her least scandalous pair of white undergarments, Alma needed all her focus to not be overwhelmed by the wet and the chill. But the pain in her fists trumped the cold she was feeling. Somehow it still was joyous. The one release to the pain was smacking Mr. Liu's open palm. The pain grew greater with each hit, the skin flaying off her knuckles, but it only made her want to draw back and strike again all the faster.

"Hiss! Hiss! Hiss!" said Alma, over and over again. Each hit was a release. Each hit was a joy. Each hit made her heart purr, that warm foretelling buzz cracking open into something else. No thoughts about being a proper lady. No thoughts about men and how to please them. The fury had moved to her fists, and the despair had taken a look at this new lady and fled. Was Alma perfectly at peace? The skin flayed off her knuckles. She punched.

"OK, so you are not ready but today I will teach you the hook punch," said Mr. Liu. "I only do this because you asked me to teach you Muay Thai, and I don't want you to become restless, and convinced you don't need to train. I am giving you gifts that will last a lifetime, how to breathe like a python and stalk like a cat, but apparently that is not enough for you. Still I want to...condescend to you. Is that the right phrase?"

"Sure," said Alma. She was working too hard at not shivering to rise to the bait. And Mr. Liu, damn him, seemed impervious to the weather, every so often merely slicking the rain off his shoulders like it was wayward dirt. And the man in the tree's sole compensation was to sing even louder.

over seas and over mounnnnn---tainnnnnnns
my body aches for dear May-Linnnngggg...

Alma noticed the knuckles on both her hands were bloody. She wiped them casually on the hem of her undergarment, each raw knuckle stinging her like a hornet. Still she admired them, like they were gaudy rings.

"Ah, do not worry," said Mr. Liu, seeing the blood. "After a while your new skin will know to grow strong, and your nerve endings will die. After awhile. So the hook punch is your stinger, the complement to your one-two. The hook punch is the knock-out drag-down motherfucking riot punch. I shall now demonstrate..."

Over seas and over mounnnnn---tainnnnnnns...

Maybe it was the weather making her lip-courageous, maybe it was something else, but Alma could stand the singing no longer.

"Mr. Liu? I make a humble request. Your companion's singing is so magnificent I am worried I might break down in tears at any moment. Might he shut his trap for awhile?"

A smile blossomed on Mr. Liu's face. He turned to the tree. "Do you hear that, you old fool? Your singing is disturbing this young woman. She demands you stop, now and forever!"

Only a blessed silence descended upon the bottom of the hillside.

Mr. Liu turned back to Alma, still smiling. "We may hear gentle sobbing, but it will be worth it. I feel great relief that you finally spoke up, Miss Alma. My Korean companion has many gifts. Singing is not one of them. And so, the hook punch..."

Alma immediately took to it. The hook was set up already by her one-two, all she needed to do was snap her heel and her hips and her shoulders to the left and *WAM!* her right fist shot out from her cheek like a piston, smashing against Mr. Liu's open palm.

"Ah, very good!" said Mr. Liu. "You see how your hook is set up by your long punch? Like a rubber band snapping. Now keep punching forever, until I say stop."

"Okey-dokey."

Alma's fists were a riotous blur. Her hips and her shoulders and her arms snapped back and forth as her right fist connected with Mr. Liu's open palm, then her left, then her right. Her heart was hissing open. She was a python, and this was her sting. She was a songbird, and this was her song.

But she had to keep punching. The flame in her fists rose higher, her flayed knuckles connecting with Mr. Liu's open palms again and again. Alma was losing steam. Her arms felt like heavy jelly, and she was having trouble keeping her fists at her cheeks. Each time her arms wandered downward Mr. Liu would rap her on the ear. After the tenth or twelfth or twentieth time Alma was madder than a march hare.

"Would you quit that?" asked Alma, too tired to phrase it graciously.

"Quit what?" said Mr. Liu, and he did it again, rapping the side of his fist against Alma's left ear.

"You know what, mister."

"Ah. Well, don't drop your fists! You are letting your guard down, Miss Alma. Never let your guard down."

"Look Mr. Liu, I know all about keeping my guard up. It's just that..."

"No buts," snapped Mr. Liu. "No excuses. There are no excuses in a battle. One side simply overcomes the other. If you lose, then your skills were not good enough. You Americans are full of excuses. And apologies. And good intentions gone bad. In my country things either are or aren't. So hit again, Miss Alma. And keep those lily-white arms of yours up."

Alma took a deep breath. Her arms felt like lead. Her hands were covered in blood. Still she raised them.

"Good," said Mr. Liu as Alma punched his palms, his eyes intent on her. "You have the makings of a warrior, Miss Alma. Remember, always wear the mask of fists. You only let your opponent peak at the unguarded you when a hand leaves your mask of fists to strike. And then your opponent sees the real you, and he is very scared, because he is not looking at a woman. He is looking at a strong hissing animal. A motherfucking python, yes?"

"That's correct," hissed Alma between punches.

Mr. Liu halted her, after a time. Alma looked around at their little training ground, her eyes having trouble focusing. She understood how the brush had been cleared in a perfect circle around the willow tree. It had been ground away to nothing by feet, twisting and turning, roiling over the soil again and again, the way the almost-frozen wet dirt beneath her had churned up from her steps. Alma wiggled her toes, noted dimly that she couldn't feel anything below her ankles.

Alma looked up. While she was punching the rain had turned to whirling snow, the willow tree sloughing it off in big wet chunks. She found some flakes in her hair. All else had ceased to exist while she was striking, the weather and the landscape and the man in the tree. She looked for him, saw some snow lay on his shoulders, and he was jiggling his dangling legs. Alma stood there and breathed. She felt her bloody fists start to rise up on their own accord, so used to punching that the muscles didn't know how to rest. Alma clasped them behind her back.

"Mr. Liu, I got a question."

"What is it, my dear?"

Alma took a breath. It was interesting how exhausted she could be, yet she could still stand and talk like a normal person. It made her wonder what else she could do. "So even if I am wearing the mask of fists, you can still strike me. So my question is: how do I block your strikes?"

"Ah, this is a very good question!" said Mr. Liu. "But I thought you just wanted to punch things, Miss Alma?"

Alma shrugged, still in her fighter's stance. Mr. Liu smiled.

"Very well. Perhaps the time has come for a demonstration." Mr. Liu turned towards the dangling legs in the tree. "Bong-ho!"

The man in the tree stopped the jiggling of his legs.

"Bong-ho, come down from there. Let's give this nice lady a demonstration of our skills."

"No," said Bong-ho, his voice deep and scratched, "Can't you see I am busy? I am enjoying myself in the tree."

"Ah," said Mr. Liu, turning to Alma. "This is very common. You see, all Koreans are lazy. It is why they get invaded alternately by either Japan or my country. When Koreans see an invading army, they shrug their shoulders and go back to foraging for garlic."

"That's a lie!" bellowed Bong-ho. "Korea has a rich and multitudinous culture!"

"Ah but what I'm saying is true. All Koreans are lazy dogs. I know, I live with you. You shit in the corner if you are not let outside every thirty minutes, and at night you dream of chasing endless wagon trains with your tongue out."

"At night I dream of murdering you, and perhaps tonight I will!"

Mr. Liu took a step towards the tree and stage whispered, "You are a garlic-eater. I know."

The Korean man swung down from the tree. Alma saw how thick-set and wild-looking he was, with long scraggly hair hanging almost to his eyes.

Mr. Liu assumed his fighting stance. Bong-ho went behind the tree and grabbed the ax. Alma took a few steps back.

"How dare you," said Bong-ho, giving the ax a test swipe. "I am a beautiful man with heartfelt desire. It is you who eats the garlic."

"Come at me, garlic-eater," whispered Mr. Liu, his arms raised.

Bong-ho charged. The wind picked up, tossing horizontal snow into the rapidly diminishing space between the two combatants. Bong-ho swung at Mr. Liu wildy, trying to chop the smaller man in half with each swing. Mr. Liu ducked and dodged, always just a hair's breadth from the ax's glinting blade. Alma wasn't sure she could ever move that fast, or with such grace. It was like a fixed dance, only she knew both were making it up as they went along, each reacting to the other in the microseconds between movements.

"You see, Miss Alma," said Mr. Liu calmly as he ducked and dodged, "I can use my toes to retreat and pounce away from any attack. I can also"—Mr. Liu ducked to avoid being beheaded—"move my head like a sneaky snake if the attacks are too close. Always be just out of reach of your attacker, so that you might in turn attack when the time is right." Mr. Liu stopped, clasped his arms behind his back. Bong-ho raised his ax and smiled wide. "I have you now, you filthy Chinese rat!" bellowed the Korean man.

"That's enough now, Bong-ho," said Mr. Liu as he watched the blade descend to his forehead.

Bong-ho froze as he was about to complete his swing. He scowled, looking as though he had a great treat taken away from him. The two combatants clasped their hands to their foreheads and bowed to one another. Alma caught Bong-ho murmuring, "I was just about to get you."

"That, I think, is adequate for today, Miss Alma," said Mr. Liu. "Would you like to stay for tea? Bong-ho makes an excellent cup."

"Oh yes please stay for tea, Miss Alma!" said Bong-ho, dropping the ax and turning toward her, "And I am very pleased to meet you."

The fire warmed Alma's bones. The tea was strong and dark and calming. Alma held her cast-iron cup with both hands, the cup's warmth compensating for the encroaching cold just outside the flames. The snow had ceased, but the chill remained.

The three sat on cut logs, huddled around the low flames. Bong-ho reached into the fire and plucked the steaming teapot from the coals. It was mid-morning: Alma knew she had to get back, wake her boy and take care of her girls and tally the amounts of liquor consumed the previous evening. She could stay a little longer though. Things were simple here.

When he was pouring her tea, Bong-ho had taken one look at Alma's bloody fist and began cursing Mr. Liu in his own language. He then produced a war bag, took out a glass jar of white salve and shyly asked Alma to hold out her hands. Up close, Alma marveled at Bong-ho's eyes, how kind they were, how his enormous calloused hands so gently rubbed the salve into her knuckles, though the salve stung worse than any punch. Still it was soothing to be taken care of, for once.

"I cannot believe you let this nice lady's hands get in such a state, you filthy Chinese rat," said Bong-ho, addressing Mr. Liu from across the fire. "He is so mean sometimes, is he not Miss Alma?"

Alma gave Bong-ho a sly wink.

"Tomorrow I shall bring you some leather gloves," continued Bong-ho. He glanced at her freezing bare feet. "And some good leather moccasins. Did you know it is quite cold out here, my dear?"

"Tomorrow, if she comes," said Mr. Liu, and he poked the fire with a stick.

"Oh yes that's right," said Bong-ho. "How is your morning soreness these days, Miss Alma?"

"Well I'll be honest, even after the stretching each morning I still feel like a snake is trying to choke me out at my rib-cage," said Alma.

Bong-ho turned to his companion. Mr. Liu shrugged, his eyes on the fire. "The greater the warrior, the later the breaking point. I wanted to see what hers was."

"Oh, did you hear the great compliment he gave you, Miss Alma?" said Bong-ho, rolling his eyes. "What a comfort that compliment will be, as your body breaks down. Tomorrow morning before the lesson I shall teach you some Qi-gong." Bong-ho grasped Alma's hand. "It will make your muscles purr."

"Tomorrow, if she comes," said Mr. Liu.

Bong-ho tsk-ed Mr. Liu. Alma couldn't hide her amusement.

The three shared a comfortable silence around the fire. Alma finished her tea, and Bong-ho got busy preparing the second steeping.

"Tell me Miss Alma, why do you want to learn Muay Thai?" asked Mr. Liu. Alma looked up to see his dark dancing eyes on her, the flames tickling beneath.

The gracious lady in her took over. "Well I don't rightly know," she said. "I do get fanciful notions sometimes."

"You are very good at blocking attacks, Miss Alma," said Mr. Liu. "But please, just take a breath and tell me."

Alma did. She let the words escape her before anything could get in their way.

"All day long, I take care of people. My gals at the dance hall, my customers, my boy. Even my ex-old man before he left town, and may he stay gone forever. I'm good at taking care of people. It's a horrible affliction. 'Cause it don't leave an iota of room for yourself. Any thought, any desire I have, it don't matter. It makes me angry, when I have the luxury to sort out my feelings. It's worse than anger though...it's rage. It festers in me, 'cause I can't let it out. Then the fury turns to despair, and it starts tumbling. I call it the mad and the bad."

"The mad and the bad?" pronounced Mr. Liu.

"That's right. The mad is the fury. The bad is the despair. One follows the other, and both just roil inside me with nowhere to go." As she said the words, Alma realized she had never spoken them aloud before. It felt good, to let them out. "At first I tried to bury 'em. Of course they still rose up, especially my mad. Just before I met you two I nearly jammed a broken beer bottle down a man's throat."

The fire crackled. Bong-ho and Mr. Liu were silent, listening. "I'm better now though," concluded Alma in a small voice. The words felt strange to say. Perhaps because she meant them.

"Ah," said Mr. Liu, and his eyes brightened. "I believe I understand. You have much venom in you. That is OK, in fact it is good.

"Venom?" spat Alma, and she made an unbecoming face.

"You say fury, I say venom. You, Miss Alma, are a motherfucking python, correct?"

"That is correct," said Alma, and she perked up on her log.

"All snakes have venom. All the best warriors too. You must get the venom out through your fists, or it will poison you. Tell me, have you had any of the mad or bad rise up since you started training?"

Alma shrugged. "Nothing sizeable."

"Ah, so the venom is being released. Just don't stop training, Miss Alma. I have seen too many would-be warriors make that mistake. They think they have summited the mountain, but really they have only taken their first steps. They convince themselves they are okey-dokey, cured of whatever it is that brought them to train. It is why I am always skeptical, if you will come tomorrow. When the pain becomes too much, many forget that it is the very pain that makes them better. Happiness is not running through a field, Miss Alma. Happiness is climbing a mountain."

"But running through fields is fun too," added Bong-ho.

It was Mr. Liu's turn to roll his eyes at Bong-ho. "Just remember that there is no culmination, Miss Alma. No summit. The venom needs to be released, constantly. You are better now than you were, and you will be better still. That is all."

The three stared into the fire a while longer. Bong-ho refilled their cups. Alma knew she had to go; still she wanted to stay.

"It's a nice thing, to talk to both of you," said Alma.

"Oh?" said Bong-ho, and he perked up on his log. "Do you have no one to talk to, Miss Alma?"

"Just my three-year-old and my employees. I don't like opening up my innards to people. They tend to make 'em more bruised."

"Oh no, Miss Alma," said Bong-ho, and he gravely shook his head. "Even I have this filthy Chinese rat to share companionship with. He is a poor listener, and he often laughs at me whenever I muster up the courage to share my problems. Still I find it's nice, to share."

"Sounds healthy," said Alma.

"Yes," nodded Bong-ho. "And I get my revenge when I laugh at how pitiful and small his own problems are."

Mr. Liu winked at her from across the fire.

"I do worry though," said Alma, "Just so long as we're still on the subject of me and my feelings, that with the venom in my fists I'll want to punch everything that makes me mad. Maybe I could get away with that if I was a man, and be lauded as some do-goodin' vengeance-maker. But I'm a lady. I run a business, and I'm a mother. I can't afford no rampages."

"It must be hard, to be a lady," grunted Bong-ho as he stared into the fire.

Mr. Liu looked at Alma from across the flames. "You are learning to fight, Miss Alma. But strangely, this often leads to less fighting in your future. It has to do with knowing in your bones that you can beat the motherfucking shit out of a person, when you first look them in the eyes. I personally enjoy this feeling very much."

"Me too," added Bong-ho.

Alma smiled at both of them. Who were these men, to listen so well to a woman's problems? The madam in her wanted to know.

"Well enough of me yappin'. I'd love to hear more about you, Mr. Liu. And you too, Bong-ho."

Mr. Liu and Bong-ho exchanged a glance. "Are you really interested, Miss Alma?" said Mr. Liu, "Or are you being polite? I cannot read Americans well enough to tell."

"I am truly interested, Mr. Liu," said Alma, and she gave him her best inquiring smile. It was nice not having to force it. "I know I complain about it enough, but I do like running a dance hall, hearing people's stories over a round of whiskey. Tell me yours. How did you learn Muay Thai? Or are all Chinese people taught it?"

Mr. Liu looked at her long. "No, Miss Jensen. I learned Muay Thai from the Thai people, when I served in the Chinese army. My Korean friend also was forced to serve, in the Japanese army. We have spent long nights around the campfire, trying to determine if we were ever in the same battles, and what we would have done to each other if we had been. Because I served in the army I was trained in various forms of Kung Fu."

"Is that how you people fight, hand to hand? It sounds so noble."

Mr. Liu looked at her long. "No, Miss Jensen. Like all people, we fight with guns and cannons and swords whenever possible. The Chinese have the dubious distinction of inventing gunpowder, and the firearm. But what discipline does it take to pull the trigger? What happens, when you run out of ammo? And what about training your mind? And so I was trained in Kung Fu. I was the best, the fastest and the most strong, in my regiment. I felt, as a young man, that I could take on anyone in the world."

"Anyone but me," grunted Bong-ho.

"Perhaps," said Mr. Liu, stroking his hairless chin. Mr. Liu saw that Bong-ho's cup was empty, and refilled it with the still-steaming tea. "But my youthful certainty changed when my regiment was assigned to patrol Siam. I was the equivalent of a lieutenant, assigned around thirty men. We were months in, finding villages around Chang-mai and ferreting out rebels. Towards the end of our assignment we were starving in the jungle, surviving on coconut and jackfruit, making our way northward. We holed up in an old temple and waited for a re-supply."

"That night we were attacked. When we first heard them we thought we were doomed. We had only two guns and a few cracked bows between us. Luckily the Siamese were even more destitute than us. Why they attacked us in such a state I will never know. They were filthy, more like animals than men. Their ribs showed above their threadbare loincloths. Oh, but they were cunning. We had China at our backs, so we could send word northward to hurry the reinforcements. My regiment settled in for a siege.

"The brave fools kept charging at us, up the hillside. They had no weapons but spears. They killed half our men, and when they ran out of spears the Siamese charged us with only their fists. After we ran out of arrows and gunpowder we obliged them.

"It's a rare thing, to experience honor on the battlefield. One of theirs would enter the middle ground with a red-colored flag, and one of ours would go out and meet them. I was so sure our Kung Fu could overcome them. I was wrong. They fought viciously, with their fists and their elbows and their knees. It was not fancy-looking, with high flying kicks that look pretty, until the man doing the kicking gets his testicles smashed in. But it was effective. The Thais were beating us five to two when our reinforcements arrived.

"I suspect the Siamese were delaying us and waiting for their own reinforcements, ours just happened to arrive first. We imprisoned them and made our way north. But I was fascinated with their martial art. At night I unloosed their cages and had them teach us, in exchange for rice. And that is how I learned."

The fire hissed and crackled. "What happened to those soldiers you captured, Mr. Liu?" asked Alma.

Mr. Liu looked at her long. "I did my duty, Miss Jensen."

Alma looked down at her empty cup, going cold in her hands. It was past time to take her leave. "Do y'all still do your own training?" she asked.

"Every day before you arrive, Miss Alma," said Mr. Liu. "We too are still climbing the mountain."

"Aren't you two masters by now?"

"Perhaps. It is hard to tell. In Muay Thai you advance by advancing; it is a wonderful, endless process. It is not like the Japanese martial arts, where you get a pretty-colored belt and a rush of congratulations every time you learn a speck of something new."

Bong-ho spat into the fire.

"Bong-ho and I disagree on many things," said Mr. Liu, "But we are united in our hatred of the Japanese people."

"Stupid Japanese fat-heads!" yelled Bong-ho.

"In Muay Thai your rank is forever in the middle," continued Mr. Liu. "There are people who can kick your ass, and there are people whom you can kick the ass of. That is all. Seek out the people who can kick your ass, Miss Alma. That is how you advance."

Alma caught a glimmer of sun through the gray. It was well on its way to high noon. "I got one last question, Mr. Liu. What are you getting out of teaching me? I'm a woman, and not of your kind. Aren't you taking a risk, teaching me?"

"Oh, perhaps another time we can talk about that," said Mr. Liu, and for the first time he evaded her eyes. "I imagine you need to get back."

Alma raised her brows. "Now who's blocking an attack, Mr. Liu?"

Mr. Liu looked long into the fire. His dark eyes were still. "Very well. When I came to this country, I did well. Prospecting. And what is more rare, I wasn't cheated out of my money. After awhile, I was able to send for my wife and daughter. I received word that they arrived in San Francisco. And then nothing. I journeyed there, on a rail line my countrymen were unfortunate enough to construct. I went to the police. I hired private detectives. I searched and searched, but I never heard a whisper. Most likely they were taken by bandits, some dark alley on some dark night. San Francisco has many dark alleys, Miss Alma. I have lost much sleep, in wondering how exactly it happened. The one thing that tortures me most of all: why didn't I ever teach them to fight? In China it is just as improper to teach women as it is here, but I could have. Perhaps it never would have made a difference, in that dark alley on that dark night. But perhaps it could have."

Mr. Liu's face betrayed a deep grief.

"I'm sorry that happened, Mr. Liu," said Alma, and there was no need to counterfeit her words.

"You remind me of her, of my daughter. She too would have made a great warrior. If I could have trained her."

Alma bowed her head. "Thank you, Mr. Liu. And I am honored to be trained by you."

Alma knew enough about men to let a respectful silence ensue. The three watched the fire crackle and die down. No one bothered to throw another log on. Alma was just about to take her leave when Bong-ho started coughing loudly.

Alma turned to him, took in his kind eyes nearly buried beneath all that dark wild hair. "And what's your story, Bong-ho?"

"Oh you don't want to hear my story, Miss Alma."

"Now stop that. I remember you said once that you were a beautiful man with heartfelt desire. I know the former is true, but what about the latter?"

Bong-ho blushed and looked away.

"Bong-ho is surprisingly shy sometimes," said Mr. Liu. "He prefers playing the pigeon-holed sing-song man. It helps him blend in more, or so he thinks."

"I am afraid in the end you will laugh at me," muttered Bong-ho into the fire.

"I promise I won't laugh," said Alma.

"Be careful what you promise, Miss Alma," said Mr. Liu.

"Very well. If you insist then I will tell," said Bong-ho, and he took a sip of tea and cleared his throat. "I was brought to this country from Japan, as little more than a slave. We were meant to be expendable workers in the Japanese-owned mines, me and the dozen Koreans with me. When we set sail the Japanese captain heard there were Koreans aboard, and he locked us in the cargo hold. Conditions were...unpleasant. My travel-mates began to die. I too was in failing health, my stomach bloated and my arms covered in scabs. One day as I was nodding off I found myself singing a song. I had never sung it before, but I was thinking about my dear wife May-Ling and the words escaped my throat. I never realized singing could be so releasing! The song revived me. It revived my companions too; I taught them the song, and together we sang. The Japanese on the ship, they hated our song. This brought me great pleasure. The captain knew too many of us had died already, so he couldn't kill us. Eventually we were gagged, but the song was already in me. I could hum and be content. This I did, over and over. Now, I sing to honor my fallen companions. I sing to honor my wife, who I will never see again. But most of all I sing because it is fun. And now Miss Alma, I make a humble request."

"What's that, Bong-ho?"

"I want to sing my song at your dance hall, on the stage. With a full band backing me. And everyone in town listening to my song and dancing and then clapping at the end and maybe throwing their hats in the air. It is why I have been practicing so much. That would be a triumphant moment for me, would it not?"

Alma saw Mr. Liu's eyes flash at her. "Okey-dokey," said Alma, and it took all of her experience as a madam to keep her face neutral.

Alma trained, never missing a day. She made it up the hill without touching her heel. "Ah, you have not failed," said Mr. Liu upon her return. "Tomorrow do two hills. If you come."

The leather gloves Bong-ho brought her gave Alma's knuckles time to heal, and the Qi-gong banished nearly all of her soreness. The moccasins too kept the frostbite at bay. After awhile Alma got so strong Mr. Liu requested she bring a pillow to punch. That didn't last long, the feathers flying out and mixing with the snow and the sweat on the ground.

One day she arrived to find a straw man hanging from the willow's branches. "Look, it is a man for you to punch," said Mr. Liu. "Bong-ho made it. He is very proud of it."

"Do you mind if I dress it?" asked Alma May.

Mr. Liu shrugged his shoulders. The next time Alma brought some of her ex-man's clothes. She felt a deep satisfaction every time she punched and kicked and grappled with that straw man and his stupid hat and red kerchief and fringed chaps.

Something kept her coming back, to the willow tree each day. She still felt the mad and the bad in her, only now they were working for her. Alma was forever wondering if she was now at peace. Perhaps, just so long as she punched.

The weather got worse. Alma trudged through a foot of snow to get to the willow tree. Always the circle around the willow was clear. Always Mr. Liu was kneeling, and Bong-ho was in the tree. Always her heart sang and it was very painful and the venom was released and it was just plain fun.

Alma got better. She learned to kick. She learned to use her knees. She learned to be the sneaky snake, to duck her head like a slithering python. The straw man was flying apart. One day when Alma arrived she saw Mr. Liu tying it to the tree.

"But Mr. Liu, won't my venomed fists and high flying kicks injure the willow tree?" asked Alma.

Mr. Liu rapped his knuckles against the tree. "Fuck this tree. If it falls under your might then that is the tree's fault."

One day when Alma arrived she saw Mr. Liu and Bong-ho tussling on the ground. "What are you two doing?" asked Alma, wondering if she should break it up the way she would a catfight at her place.

Mr. Liu was released from Bong-ho's choke-hold. "Just having a friendly disagreement," said Mr. Liu, massaging his throat.

"I won," muttered Bong-ho. "The spirit of Yi Sun-shin moved me. He is clearly the superior general."

"Was that another martial art, what y'all were doing?"

"Yes, Miss Alma. It is a form of Japanese wrestling called jujutsu. Bong-ho learned it in the Japanese army. He is, I must concede, a master."

"Looks useful," said Alma May.

"Oh it is, Miss Alma. Many fights end on the ground. To only know a standing martial art is very incomplete. It also helps to train with a weapon. I use short butterfly swords and Bong-ho, perhaps to your unsurprise, trains with an ax."

"I want to learn," said Alma.

"Want to learn what, Miss Alma?"

"All of it."

"Well," said Mr. Liu, studying her, "tomorrow, when you come, we can begin."

That pig-customer came back to Alma's place, one inauspicious Tuesday night. Alma couldn't help but watch him from the end of the bar. The pig-man took Alma's brazen watching for something else, and approached.

The band was playing a rousing rendition of "John Henry's Hammer." The people dancing stomped their feet, ladies on one side, gents on the other. The bouncer gave Alma a look, but she waved him away.

"Hi, I'm Mitch," said the pig-man. He stunk of rotten apple cores, and his hare-lip was covered in pink sweat.

No look of recognition crossed his face. Alma flashed her teeth, wider.

"Care for a dance? I'm quite nimble on my feet." And the pig-man pounded his flat feet on her floor. Alma shook her head, slowly.

The pig-man was unfazed. He leaned closer, his greasy brown hair swinging against his shoulders. "You know, you're quite pretty for being the oldest gal in the place," said the pig-man. "Are you thinking what I'm thinking?" And his pig-eyes gleamed.

"Boy I hope so," said Alma.

The pig-man bent closer, his mouth near her ear. She worked to not recoil from his breath.

"You know, I spy a little closet over there. What say you and I..."

The man reached for Alma's behind. She rotated her forearm and batted his pig-hand away, still smiling. It happened so fast the pig-man only looked confused.

"Hey, what's the story, sweetheart?"

Alma put her right foot forward, her left back. The pig-man's little eyes darted around the room.

"You know, I ain't one to be messed with," said the pig-man. "You ain't heard the name Wild Mitch Jackson before?"

Alma shook her head. Slowly.

"Well, I'm an outlaw. I got this here pistol, and I'm a..."

Alma just stared at him. The pig-man's little eyes had a gloss to them, like tears could form if things didn't go his way.

It was Alma's turn to lean close. "Here's the story, Wild Mitch. Gun or not, if I ever see your snout in my place again I'll punch it so hard it'll lodge into your little pig brain. Are we clear on that, you outlaw?"

Mitch recoiled as though Alma had struck him. Alma cracked her knuckles. She was close enough, and fast enough, where his gun wouldn't matter. It looked like Mitch could intuit it.

"You're so mean," said Mitch, and Alma caught awe in his voice. She held her stance.

After awhile of staring, the band still playing and the people dancing and the folks around them guzzling their drinks, Mitch hurried out. Alma watched him leave, let out her breath, shook out her fists and went to the other side of the bar, remembering to use only her toes.

About Etchings Press

Etchings Press is a student-run publisher at the University of Indianapolis that runs a post-publication award—the Whirling Prize—as well as an annual publication contest for one poetry chapbook, one prose chapbook, and one novella. On occasion, Etchings Press publishes new chapbooks from previous winners. The press is the new home for the Floodgate Poetry Series. For more information about these contests, the Whirling Prize post-publication award, and the Floodgate Poetry Series, please visit etchings.uindy.edu.

Previous winners and publications:

Poetry

2021: *My Mother's Ghost Scrubs the Floor at 2 a.m.*
   by Robert Okaji
2020: *Vaginas Need Air* by Tori Grant Welhouse
2019: *As Lovers Always Do* by Marne Wilson
2018: *In the Herald of Improbable Misfortunes*
   by Robert Campbell
2017: *Uncle Harold's Maxwell House Haggadah*
   by Danny Caine
2016: *Some Animals* by Kelli Allen
2015: *Velocity of Slugs* by Joey Connelly
2014: *Action at a Distance* by Christopher Petruccelli

Prose

2021: *Bad Man Love Stories* by Curtis VanDonkelaar (fiction)

2020: *Three in the Morning and You Don't Smoke Anymore* by Peter J. Stavros (fiction)

2019: *Dissenting Opinion from the Committee for the Beatitudes* by Marc J. Sheehan (fiction)

2018: *The Forsaken* by Chad V. Broughman (fiction)

2017: *Unravelings* by Sarah Cheshire (memoir)

2016: *Pathetic* by Shannon McLeod (essays)

2015: *Ologies* by Chelsea Biondolillo (essays)

2014: *Static: Stories* by Frederick Pelzer (fiction)

Novella

2021: *Miss Alma May Learns to Fight* by Stuart Rose

2020: *Under Black Leaves* by Doug Ramspeck

2019: *Savonne, Not Vonny* by Robin Lee Lovelace

2018: *Edge of the Known Bus Line* by James R. Gapinski

2017: *The Denialist's Almanac of American Plague and Pestilence* by Christopher Mohar

2016: *Followers* by Adam Fleming Petty

Chapbooks from Previous Winners

2020: *Fruit Rot* by James R. Gapinski (fiction)

2016: *#LOVESONG* by Chelsea Biondolillo (microessays with photos and found text)

Stuart Rose is an MFA student at the Rainier Writing Workshop at Pacific Lutheran University. He is employed by the U.S. Forest Service as a seasonal trails worker and enjoys playing his guitar so loudly that it wakes up his cat. Stuart lives and works in Montana.